First American Edition. Copyright ©1995 The Walt Disney
Company. All rights reserved under international
copyright conventions. Published in the United States by
Grolier Enterprises Inc., Danbury, Connecticut. Originally
published in Denmark as 101 DALMATINERE by Egmont
Gruppen, Copenhagen. ISBN: 0-7172-8483-2. Based on the
book by Dodie Smith, published by Viking Press.
Manufactured in the United States of America.
F G H   6 7 8 9

Once there were two Dalmatians named Pongo and Perdita. They lived in a snug little house in London.

Their pets, Anita and Roger Radcliff, lived with them.

Nanny, the housekeeper, took care of them all.
One day Pongo got some wonderful news.
Perdita was going to have puppies!
Everyone was very happy.

At last the big day arrived.
"The puppies are here!" Nanny cried.
"How many?" asked Roger.

"Eight," Nanny replied.
"No," shouted Anita from the other room. "Eleven! Wait! Fifteen!"

Fifteen puppies!
Perdita was
very proud.

"Pongo, you old
rascal," said Roger.
He thought the
puppies were
wonderful.

"They'll get their spots when they're a little
bigger," Nanny told him.

Suddenly there was a clap of thunder. In swept Anita's old friend Cruella De Vil. Her long fur coat trailed behind her.

"I see the puppies are here at last," she said. "I'll buy them all."

"They're not for sale!" replied Roger. "You'll be sorry!" Cruella snapped as she stormed off. Pongo and Perdita were happy to see her leave.

But Cruella wasn't finished. "They can't stop me," she cackled.

Cruella hired Horace and Jasper Badun to steal the puppies. "As soon as you have a chance, sneak into their house and grab those puppies," she told them.

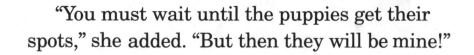

"You must wait until the puppies get their spots," she added. "But then they will be mine!"

Each day, the puppies grew bigger. And each day, they got more spots!

The puppies liked watching television. The show they liked the most was about a dog named Thunderbolt.

"Get 'em, Thunderbolt!" shouted Penny.

"Time for bed," Pongo said when the show ended.

"Aw, Dad, we're not sleepy," said Lucky.

After the puppies went to bed, Pongo and
Perdita went to the park. They took Roger and
Anita with them.

But as soon as they went out, Horace and
Jasper went in!

Jasper locked
Nanny in the attic.
Horace put all the
puppies into a big
sack. They took all
fifteen puppies!

When Roger and Anita returned, Nanny told them what had happened. Roger called the police. But the police couldn't find the puppies. Perdita and Pongo were very upset.

Then Pongo had an idea. "Let's try the Twilight Bark," he said. "It's our only hope." "All right," agreed Perdita.

Pongo barked in a special code.

"Yap and yip and yelp, yelp, yelp!
Fifteen puppies need your help!
Calling all hounds,
yippers and yappers.
Please help us find
their cruel kidnappers!"

The message was
passed from dog to dog.
It woke up Towser, a
bloodhound who lived
way out in the country.

"Hmmph!" growled Towser to Lucy the goose. "A message from the city. An important one, too! I'd better tell the folks on the farm."

Old Towser's barking woke up a cat named Sergeant Tibs.

Tibs told
Captain, a horse,
to awaken a
sheepdog named
Colonel.

The Colonel
pricked up his
ears. "Fifteen
spotted puddles were stolen!"

"I think that's *puppies*, sir," said Sergeant Tibs.

Tibs remembered hearing some barking at the old De Vil place.

"Nonsense! That house has been empty for years," said the Colonel.

"Not any longer," Captain answered. "There's smoke rising from the chimney."

"Then we'd better investigate, Tibs," barked the Colonel. They went to the old house.

Sergeant Tibs slipped into the house.
What a surprise!
He saw ninety-nine Dalmatian puppies!
Fifteen of them were huddled in front of the TV.
"Those must be the ones!" Tibs said. He
raced back to tell the others.

The Colonel
sent a message.
Dog by dog, the
message was
passed from the
country to the
city.

"Listen, Perdy!" said Pongo. "It's the Great
Dane. He has an answer for us."
The two Dalmatians raced to meet the big dog.

"The puppies
have been found at
the De Vil place,"
the Great Dane
said.

"We must go at
once!" cried Perdita.

When they got
to the country,
Sergeant Tibs and
the Colonel were
waiting for them.

"Follow us," said Sergeant Tibs. "There's no time to waste!"

They sneaked into the old house.

"What does Cruella want with all these puppies?" they heard Jasper ask.

"She says she's going to make them into a coat," Horace answered.

"A dog-skin coat?" cried Perdita. "How cruel!"

She counted the puppies. "Pongo!" she whispered. "There are ninety-nine puppies here!"

"We must take them all home with us," Pongo replied. "Let's go."

Sergeant Tibs led the way. Horace and Jasper didn't see them leave. They were too busy watching television!

The Dalmatians followed Tibs to the barn.
But they weren't safe yet.

Horace and Jasper had finally noticed the
puppies were gone. They were following their
tracks in the snow!

"Here they come!" shouted Tibs. "We'd
better do something."

"We'll hold them off," Captain told Pongo.

The Dalmatians escaped out the back door.
And Captain gave the Baduns a swift kick
when they came through the front door!

Pongo and Perdita led the puppies through a snowstorm.

Suddenly Pongo heard a car. "Quick, hide!" he urged. The dogs hid under a bridge.

Luckily Horace and Jasper didn't see them.

Pongo decided to walk along the frozen stream. That way, Horace and Jasper couldn't follow their tracks.

Home seemed very far away!

"My nose is froze!" whimpered Lucky. "And
my tail is froze! And my toes are froze!"

All the puppies were tired and hungry.

Just then Pongo heard a friendly bark.

"Follow me," said a collie. "I have a place for
you to stay."

The collie led them to a warm barn.

Some friendly cows gave the puppies plenty of milk to drink.

Soon ninety-nine puppies were fast asleep in the hay.

Pongo and Perdita thanked the cows and the collie.

"Tomorrow morning you can go to the village," said the collie. "A Labrador retriever will meet you there. He'll show you how to get home."

The next morning Pongo and Perdita continued on their way.

Pongo knew that Cruella would be looking for them.

He tried to brush away their tracks with a branch.

But Cruella saw the tracks. "They're headed for the village!" she shrieked.

When the dogs reached the village, the Labrador was waiting for them. He led them to an empty blacksmith's shop.

"I've got a ride for you," he said. "A van is leaving for London soon. There's room for all of you."

But Cruella and her men
had reached the village, too.
Cruella was angry with Horace and Jasper.
"Find them! Find them now!" she shouted.
"Pongo, how will we get to the van?" Perdita
whispered.

Just then Lucky said, "Patch pushed me!"
He was covered with soot.

"He pushed me first!" Patch whined. He was
covered with soot, too.

That gave Pongo an idea.

He rolled in the soot. "Look! I'm a Labrador. Come on, Perdy. Let's all be Labradors!"

Soon all the Dalmatians were covered in soot.

"We're going to fool the nasty lady!" the pups giggled.

n was getting ready to leave.
r hurry," said the Labrador.
y one the puppies got
he van. They
lost made it!

But the last puppy got stuck
in the snow.
   The snow washed off the soot.

"There they are!" Cruella cried.
The van pulled away in the nick of time!

"After them!" Cruella shouted.

Cruella drove
too fast for the
slippery road.
  "Watch out!"
cried Horace.

But it was too
late. Cruella's car
tumbled down a
hill. Everyone
landed in the
deep, soft snow.
  But the car was
smashed to pieces!

Back in London, Anita and Nanny were decorating the Christmas tree. Roger was too upset to help.

"I miss Pongo and Perdy so much!" said Anita.

"I know," answered Nanny. "Sometimes, at night, I think I hear them bark. But it always turns out to be a dream."

"Wait!" cried Anita. "Did you hear that bark?"

Nanny flung open the door. A large black dog jumped on Roger and covered him with kisses and s̶

"It's Pongo and Perdita with their little ones!" cried Nanny. She began to dust off the puppies.

Then Anita and Roger noticed the room was filled with dogs.

All in all, there were one hundred and one Dalmatians!

"Whatever shall we do with them?" Anita asked.

"We'll buy a big place in the country," said Roger. "A Dalmatian Plantation!"

It was a very merry Christmas, after all.